the CRITTER club

:: Liz and the Nosy Neighbor ::

by Callie Barkley ♥ illustrated by Tracy Bishop

LITTLE SIMON
New York London Toronto Sydney New Delhi

LITTLE SIMON

An imprint of Simon & Schuster Children's Publishing Division · 1230 Avenue of the Americas, New York, New York 10020 · First Little Simon paperback edition September 2018 · Copyright © 2018 by Simon & Schuster, Inc. All rights reserved, including the right of reproduction in whole or in part in any form. LITTLE SIMON is a registered trademark of Simon & Schuster, Inc., and associated colophon is a trademark of Simon & Schuster, Inc. For information about special discounts for bulk purchases, please contact Simon & Schuster Special Sales at 1-866-506-1949 or business@simonandschuster.com. The Simon & Schuster Speakers Bureau can bring authors to your live event. For more information or to book an event contact the Simon & Schuster Speakers Bureau at 1-866-248-3049 or visit our website at www.simonspeakers.com. Designed by Laura Roode. The text of this book was set in ITC Stone Informal Std.
Manufactured in the United States of America 0818 MTN
10 9 8 7 6 5 4 3 2 1
Cataloging-in-Publication Data for this title is available from the Library of Congress.
ISBN 978-1-5344-2969-7 (hc)
ISBN 978-1-5344-2968-0 (pbk)
ISBN 978-1-5344-2970-3 (eBook)

Table of Contents

Chapter 1

Art Is Everywhere

Liz Jenkins opened her locker. She reached inside and unzipped her backpack.

Her best friend Ellie Mitchell appeared at her side. "Can I see how it turned out?" Ellie asked.

The whole class had just come from the art room. They had finished their cut-paper collages—a

project they'd worked on for a few weeks. Liz was excited to take hers home.

Liz unrolled her collage.

"Another Liz Jenkins masterpiece!" Ellie said.

Liz smiled. "Aw, thanks, Ellie,"

she said. She asked to see Ellie's art. It was ablaze with reds, oranges, and yellows. "I love the colors!" Liz exclaimed.

"Me too," Ellie agreed. "But I wasn't really thinking about the pattern. Yours is so planned out."

Liz *had* put a lot of thought into the layout. She was going for a swirly, *Starry Night* look. Like Vincent Van Gogh, one of her favorite artists.

Just then, their teacher, Mrs. Sienna, poked her head into the hall-way. "Come in and let's get settled for science," she told them.

So Liz and Ellie put their artwork in their lockers. "Ellie," Liz whispered as they walked into class, "did you give Mrs. Sienna your note?"

"I almost forgot!" Ellie pulled a piece of paper out of her pocket. "I'll do it now."

Now everything was set. Liz knew that her other best friends, Marion Ballard and Amy Purvis, had handed in the notes their parents had written too. They were all coming home with Liz for a Friday night sleepover!

The girls had a lot to talk about, like stocking up on supplies at The Critter Club. That was the animal rescue shelter the four friends had started.

This week, they were going to be pet sitting some fish

called neon tetras. The Critter Club had to be ready for their guests!

But right now, Liz had to concentrate on science. Mrs. Sienna was telling them about their next science unit. It was on animal habitats.

HABITAT

Isn't that just a science-y way of saying home? Liz wondered.

Mrs. Sienna held up a shoebox. "We are going to be making animal habitat dioramas," she said. "Like this one."

Mrs. Sienna turned the box sideways to show the inside. It had been decorated to look like a flower

HABITAT

garden! A paper hummingbird was suspended by a string from one side of the box. It looked like it was hovering next to a flower.

"Each of you will choose an animal," Mrs. Sienna went on. "Any animal you wish! Then, your assignment is to create a scene of that animal in its habitat."

Liz heard the words *create* and *scene.* It made her think . . . *art*! Art and animals! Liz's two favorite things!

"So," said Mrs. Sienna, "your homework for the weekend—"

Some students groaned.

"Don't worry," Mrs. Sienna said with a smile. "All you need to do is pick your animal. On Monday, I will meet with each of you. You can tell me what you've decided."

Liz nodded. Decisions weren't always easy for her. But she could do this. She could choose an animal by Monday.

This was going to be fun!

chapter 2

Friday Is for Friends!

At dismissal, Liz's dad picked the girls up from school. They piled into the back of the Jenkins family van.

"How about pizza tonight?" Mr. Jenkins asked. "I bought some whole-wheat dough. We can make personal-size pizzas. Each of you can choose your own toppings."

"Sounds great!" said Marion.

"Yum!" said Amy.

"I love pizza!" cried Ellie.

Within minutes, they were at Liz's house. Amy noticed two big trucks parked next door. "What's going on at your neighbor's?" Amy asked.

Mr. Jenkins explained. "Oh, our old neighbors, the Wallaces,

recently moved. A new family is moving in today."

Ellie pointed at bikes parked next to one of the trucks. "One of those looks like a kid's bike!" she said.

Liz peered out the car window. Ellie was right. "Maybe it's some-one our age!" she said hopefully.

Liz led the way up to her bed-room. The girls put down their backpacks.

"What should we do first?" Liz asked them. "Snack? Game? Movie?"

Marion shook her head. "Homework first!" she said with a twinkle in her eye.

Liz, Amy, and Ellie gasped.

"On a Friday afternoon?" Amy said. "Marion, even you aren't *that* organized."

Marion laughed. "You're right," she replied. "But hey! I think I already know my animal for that science project. Zebras! I've always wondered how similar they are to horses."

Amy spoke up next. "I'm going to choose wolves," she said. "Maybe the kind that live in the Arctic."

Ellie clapped excitedly. "I want to do some kind of tropical bird," she said. "Like Lenny." That was Ellie's grandmother's pet parrot. "Something colorful," she added dreamily.

The three friends turned to Liz. "How about you?" Amy asked her.

Liz was amazed. "You all have such good ideas already!" she said.

Ellie threw an arm around Liz's shoulder. "Yeah," Ellie interrupted. "But we know your diorama will be the most artistic one!"

Amy and Marion nodded in agreement.

Liz beamed. Their faith in her made her feel so happy.

"So what animal *are* you going to choose?" Amy asked.

Liz opened her mouth to answer. And nothing came out. She didn't know! But she wanted it to be *really* good. Her friends were expecting the best.

Just then, there was a knock at the bedroom door.

Liz's mom poked her head in. "I made oatmeal cookies," she said. "Anyone hungry?"

The girls jumped up. "Yes!" Liz exclaimed.

They all headed downstairs to the kitchen. On the way, Mrs. Jenkins asked them a favor.

"I baked way too many cookies," she said. "Would you girls bring some to the new neighbors? Moving day can be exhausting,

and I thought it would be nice to offer a pick-me-up."

Liz looked at her friends. They all nodded excitedly.

"We'll go now!" Liz told her mom.

The New Neighbor

The four friends squeezed onto the front steps of the neighbors' house. Liz pressed the doorbell.

They heard a muffled *ding-dong* from inside.

They waited, listening for footsteps.

But none came. The girls waited another minute. Liz pressed the doorbell again.

Another minute passed. No one came.

"One more try?" Ellie suggested. She pressed the doorbell twice. *Ding-dong. Ding-dong.*

Liz shrugged. They turned to go. Then they heard a rush of footsteps. The lock clicked. The door opened.

"Hello?" said a woman. She was dressed in jeans and a plaid shirt. A bandana held her hair back. "I'm sorry!" she said. "Did you ring more than once? I was out in the

backyard. I guess my son didn't hear the bell."

The girls introduced themselves.

"Hi, I'm Liz. My family lives next door," she said. "And these are my friends, Amy, Marion, and Ellie. We came to say welcome to the neighborhood!"

"And her mom made some cookies," Amy said. She handed the plate to the woman.

The woman smiled at them warmly. "Thank you so much!" she said. "I'm Sylvia Knight. My husband, Michael, just ran out to the store. But let me introduce you to Dylan."

Mrs. Knight invited them in. The girls waited in the foyer while Mrs. Knight disappeared into another room.

She returned a minute later with a boy at her side. Liz thought he *did* look to be about her age!

"This is Dylan," Mrs. Knight said.

The boy smiled and gave a friendly wave.

His mom put a hand on his shoulder. "He's starting school at Santa Vista Elementary on Monday," she said.

Liz and her friends smiled at one another. "That's our school too!" Liz cried. "What grade are you in?"

"Second," Dylan replied. "I think my teacher's name is Mrs. Sienna or something?"

"Wow! You're in our class!" Marion told him.

Ellie nudged Liz. "That's cool," said Ellie. "You guys will be next-door neighbors *and* classmates!"

Mrs. Knight thanked them again for the cookies.

"See you Monday at school, Dylan!" Liz said warmly as they turned to go.

She looked back, expecting Dylan to say the same. But he was silent.

Hmm, thought Liz. Was he just kind of shy?

Or was Dylan not all that happy to have a classmate next door?

Liz's Secret

Liz had the Monday morning blues.

Sometimes that's how it was after a great weekend. She'd had fun with her friends on Friday night. On Saturday, Liz's mom took her sock shopping. She found some with polka dots and crazy stripes! And on Sunday, Liz had gone to the park with her dad and brother.

Stewart had even let Liz hit a few baseballs—usually her only job was to retrieve the balls *Stewart* hit!

Liz sighed.

She just didn't feel ready for school. She hadn't even decided on an animal for the science project! Flying squirrel? Komodo dragon? Platypus? Liz loved unique animals. But none of them seemed right.

"What did you pick?" Ellie asked as they sat down in Mrs. Sienna's classroom.

Without thinking, Liz blurted out, "You'll have to wait and see!"

She grinned as if she knew a secret.

It wasn't a lie, exactly. But it wasn't honest either.

Mrs. Sienna took attendance. As she did, there was a knock on the classroom door. She opened it and stepped into the hallway for a minute.

When she came back in, Mrs. Sienna asked for everyone's attention. "We have a new student today!" she announced.

Liz looked at Ellie, Amy, and Marion. *We know who it is,* Liz thought.

Sure enough, in walked Dylan.

Mrs. Sienna introduced him to the class. Then she assigned him the empty desk—right behind Liz.

Dylan took his seat. Liz turned around to wave. "Hi, neighbor," she whispered.

Dylan didn't smile. But maybe he was nervous. After all, it was his first day.

The class began their morning math. Later on, they went to gym. Then they had quiet reading time. During reading, Mrs. Sienna started calling students up one by one.

Uh oh, thought Liz. *She's asking everyone for their animal. Quick! Just decide! Aardvark? Narwhal? Angler fish?*

It felt even harder to choose now. Liz could hear what her classmates were saying to the teacher. Shamir was doing rattlesnakes. Olivia had picked weasels. Liz didn't want to choose an animal that someone else was doing.

Her choices were dwindling!

Just then, the lunch bell rang.

"I'll meet with the rest of you after recess," Mrs. Sienna said. "Have a good lunch!"

Liz saw her chance. She wanted to talk to Mrs. Sienna without anyone around. So she stayed seated as her classmates filed out.

When the room was quiet, Liz went up to the teacher's desk.

"Mrs. Sienna," she said nervously, "I can't give you my animal choice yet."

The teacher looked surprised.

"I've thought about it a lot," Liz added. "I just haven't come up with the perfect one."

Mrs. Sienna gave her a sympathetic smile.

"Well, Liz," she said gently, "I can give you more time. But there's no right or wrong here. Just choose an animal that interests you. We can talk about it again tomorrow. Okay?"

Liz nodded and sighed with relief.

"I'm sure you'll find your inspiration," Mrs. Sienna said. "Just keep thinking. And keep your eyes open. A great idea might be right in front of your nose!"

Liz headed for the door. As she

turned, she jumped a little, startled.

Dylan was there, sitting at his desk. He had his nose in a book. But as Liz walked out, Dylan got up. He walked over to Mrs. Sienna.

Had he been sitting there the whole time? Because if so . . .

Liz cringed.

He had heard everything.

Chapter 5

Something Smells Fishy

At lunch, Liz sat down with Amy, Marion, and Ellie. They were talking about Amy's new wildlife magazine.

Liz was glad they weren't talking about the science project. She had let Ellie think she had an animal all picked out. And now Dylan knew she didn't. Liz felt a little embarrassed.

"We were wondering where you were!" Marion said to Liz.

"I just had to tell Mrs. Sienna something," Liz said. Then she quickly changed the subject. "Oh, Ellie! Remember! It's our day at The Critter Club today."

Ellie nodded. "Right!" she replied. "I'll bring a book I checked out on aquarium pets."

Liz nodded. "And I think we need fish food. Maybe my mom can take me to the pet store after school.

Then I'll meet you at the barn and we can take care of the fish."

Mrs. Jenkins was happy to take Liz to the pet store. But first, she had to stop at the grocery store.

Walking through the seafood department, Liz held her nose. The fishy smell was a little too much.

But it brought back good memories. Like the time she and her family went to Luna Beach on vacation.

"How come I love this smell at the beach but not the store?" Liz asked her mom. "In here, it seems stinky."

Liz's mom laughed.

At the checkout counter, Liz unloaded their basket.

"Oh hi!" Mrs. Jenkins said suddenly.

Liz looked up from the groceries. Behind them in line was Mrs. Knight—and Dylan.

Liz's mom and Mrs. Knight started chatting. Dylan and Liz stood there looking at each other. At last, Liz thought of something to say.

"So how was your first day?" she asked Dylan.

He smiled. "Good, I guess," he said. "I like Mrs. Sienna."

Liz nodded. "Me too."

They fell into silence again. Then Dylan's eyebrows shot up. "So that project," he said. "Mrs. Sienna asked me to stay back at lunch so she could tell me about it."

Ah, thought Liz. *So that's why Dylan had been there.*

"What animal are you going to do?" he asked her.

Liz frowned.

Dylan already knew that she didn't know. Hadn't he heard that, loud and clear?

Wait. Was Dylan *teasing* her?

The cashier called, "Next!" Liz and her mom moved forward in line. Within minutes, they had paid. They were headed out the door.

"That Dylan seems like a nice boy," Mrs. Jenkins was saying.

Liz didn't say anything. She wasn't sure about that yet.

Chapter 6

Grains of an Idea

Liz and her mom went on to the pet store. Liz picked out some fish food.

On a nearby shelf, the glittery grains of fish tank sand caught her eye. She picked up a bag, just to admire it.

Liz smiled. It was another reminder of Luna Beach—and that fun sandcastle contest she had entered!

They paid for the fish food. Then Mrs. Jenkins dropped Liz at The Critter Club.

Ellie was already in the barn. She waved Liz over to a row of aquarium tanks. Three of them were lined up on a table.

"The neon tetras are here!" Ellie

told Liz. "Ms. Sullivan said the owner dropped them off this morning. And look! He brought *more* friends for us to watch. A red-eared slider turtle and a crayfish!"

The turtle and crayfish each had their own tanks. Liz waved through the glass to welcome the guests.

The neon tetras were tiny! But their shimmer and color made them stand out in the water.

The turtle looked like ones Liz had seen up at Marigold Lake.

And the crayfish seemed familiar too. "This guy looks like a lobster," Liz said.

Ellie nodded. "My book says they are sometimes called freshwater lobsters!"

Liz remembered finding pieces of lobster shell washed up on Luna Beach.

It was the third time she'd

thought of the beach that day. It *had* been a very memorable vaca-tion. And busy, too! Liz had spent most of that week taking care of a baby octopus that had washed ashore.

That's when it hit her.

"Right under my nose!" Liz cried out loud.

Ellie looked at her funny. "What?"

Joy and relief and excitement washed over Liz like a big ocean wave. Finally, she knew what animal to choose. And the inspiration *had* been right under her nose.

"An octopus!" Liz said to Ellie. "That's what I'm going to do for my science project."

In a rush of words, Liz told Ellie everything.

"I couldn't come up with anything," Liz explained. "When you asked me, I made it sound like I knew. But I didn't."

Ellie gave her a playful nudge. "It's no big deal," she said. "So octopus, huh? How are you going to make it?"

Liz was quiet a moment. She was thinking about the sparkly sand at the pet store.

"I think I have an idea," Liz said.

Chapter 7

Backyard Spy!

Liz sat down at a free computer. It was Tuesday—computer lab day. Amy took the computer to Liz's left. Dylan sat down to her right.

"Hi," he said to Liz.

It was the first time he'd said it first.

"Hi!" Liz replied.

Now that she'd picked an animal,

Liz felt a lot better. She'd told Mrs. Sienna her choice. She was excited to do octopus research. And she didn't feel as weird around Dylan.

They were neighbors. Shouldn't they be friends?

"Library voices in here," Mrs. Sienna reminded the class.

The room quieted down. But the sound of fingers on keyboards tapped on.

Liz typed in the address of an animal website Mrs. Sienna had

given them to do research.

As the page loaded, she sat back in her chair. She noticed Dylan talking to Joey on his other side. Dylan was whispering and pointing to something on Joey's computer. Joey nodded and whispered back.

Liz leaned over toward Dylan. "Hey. What animal did *you* decide on?" she whispered.

Dylan didn't answer. He didn't even turn to look at her.

"Dylan?" she tried again.

But he just kept on talking to Joey.

O-kay, thought Liz. *Busy, I guess?*

But then at dismissal, it happened again.

Liz had ridden her bike to school. Across the schoolyard, Liz saw Dylan at the bike rack, unlocking his own bike. Cool! They were headed to the same place.

Liz stepped up her pace. "Hi, Dylan!" she called out to him. "I'll ride with you."

Dylan didn't look up. He tucked his bike lock into his backpack. He clicked his helmet strap. Then he hopped on his bike and rode away.

"Hey!" Liz yelled as she reached the rack.

He had totally ignored her. Again!

Liz slowly pedaled home. Maybe Dylan didn't want to be friends.

Liz cheered herself up by starting on her diorama.

She found an old shoebox in her closet. It seemed like a good size for a diorama. Liz picked two shades of blue paint from her art case. She grabbed a paintbrush.

In the kitchen, she found a bag of sparkly fish tank sand next to her mom's purse. "Thanks for getting the sand, Mom!" Liz called out. It was part of Liz's plan.

"You're welcome!" Mrs. Jenkins called from upstairs.

Liz carried everything out onto their back porch. She sat down on the porch steps. She opened the paints and dipped in her brush. Liz coated the inside of the box with a thick layer of blue paint.

Then Liz opened the bag of sand. She dropped handfuls of sand into one corner of the box. That was going to be her ocean floor. The wet paint would act like glue. Later, she could shake out the extra sand.

But for now, Liz set it down to dry.

Just then, she heard a noise.

Rattle. Rattle-rattle. Liz stared at the backyard fence—the part that divided her backyard and Dylan's.

Rattle-rattle. The fence gate was rattling. Like someone was shaking it from the other side.

Liz couldn't see over the top. The fence was too high. So she put down the shoebox and paintbrush. Then she got up and walked over to the gate.

Through the gap at the gate latch, Liz could see part of a face.

There was an eye. There was a nose. Someone was peeking through the fence!

Liz reached for the latch. She flung the gate open.

Dylan fell through, into the Jenkins' backyard.

"What are you doing?" Liz cried.

Chapter 8

Not So Loud and Clear

Flat on his stomach, Dylan looked up at Liz. She loomed over him, hands on her hips.

Liz could not figure this kid out.

Ignoring her twice in one day? And just now, had he been spying on her? Or what? Liz didn't get it.

"Sorry," Dylan said sheepishly. "I was looking for my pet. Somehow she got out and I can't find her. I just thought maybe she got into your yard. I was trying to see."

A missing pet?

"What kind of pet?" Liz asked.

"A chinchilla," Dylan replied. "Her name is Nugget."

Aw, Liz thought. "That's a type of rodent, right?" she asked.

Dylan nodded. "She looks like a big mouse with *extra*-big ears," he said. "She's pretty adorable."

Liz didn't think she'd ever seen a chinchilla in real life.

"I'll help you look for her!" Liz offered.

"Really?" Dylan said. "That would be great."

They went back into Dylan's backyard and started there. They searched under shrubs. They poked around in the flower garden. They looked along the fence for signs that Nugget had tunneled out.

Dylan frowned. "Here's the thing," he said. "Chinchillas are really good climbers." He looked up and around. "We have a bunch of tall trees back here. Nugget could be . . . anywhere."

Now he sounded really worried.

"And it rained last night," Dylan continued. "Her fur isn't supposed to get wet." He looked nervously up at the sky. "Are those *more* rain clouds?"

Liz tried to calm him down. "Don't worry," she said. "I really think we'll be able to find her." Liz thought for a moment, then said, "Especially if we get more help!"

Liz explained her idea to Dylan. Then she ran home. She called Ellie, Amy, and Marion and asked if they could come help. Then she headed back to Dylan's yard to keep looking.

Within a half hour, Liz heard the doorbell—*ding dong*—through Dylan's back screen door.

"That must be them!" Liz said to Dylan.

Dylan looked at her, confused. "What?" he said.

"Your doorbell," Liz said. "I think the girls are here."

"Oh! The doorbell rang?" Dylan replied. "I'll go let them in!" He headed for the house. "I guess I didn't hear it. I can't hear much in my right ear," he added.

Liz stood frozen to her spot, thinking about what Dylan had just said.

Chapter 9

Find That Critter!

While Dylan went to let the girls in, Liz's mind was racing. Suddenly, things seemed to make so much sense!

The times she thought Dylan had ignored her? He probably just hadn't heard her, since he was turned away from her!

Liz's conversation with Mrs.

Sienna? Dylan probably didn't hear it, after all. So he *wasn't* teasing her at the grocery store.

Liz thought back to Friday. The girls brought over cookies and rang the doorbell so many times. *I guess my son didn't hear the bell*, Mrs. Knight had said.

It all made sense. Liz felt a little bad. She had jumped to conclusions about Dylan.

But now she knew better.

Dylan came out of the house, followed by Ellie, Amy, and Marion.

"Okay!" Ellie exclaimed. "Let's find this Nugget!"

Amy had brought binoculars. She aimed them up into the trees, looking for signs of the chinchilla.

Ellie searched in muddy areas for chinchilla tracks.

Marion had her clipboard. She

wrote down all the chinchilla information Dylan could think of.

"There is also that gap in the fence by the gate," Liz said. "She could have squeezed through there."

So they started searching Liz's backyard too.

"If they hate to be wet," Liz said, "then how do you give Nugget a bath?"

"I don't," Dylan said. "Nugget gives herself a bath in dust. Or sand."

Sand, thought Liz. That big bag of sand was still sitting on her back porch.

Liz hurried over, just to check it out.

The bag was just as she had left it—next to the paint and the shoebox. Liz didn't see any sign of Nugget.

Then, out of the corner of her eye, Liz saw the shoebox move.

She did a double-take. What was that?

Liz stared at the box.

It shook again! And now a small cloud of sand dust was rising out of the box.

"Guys!" Liz shouted to her

friends. "My project! My project is alive!"

Dylan and the girls came running. Liz pointed at the box. They saw it too! The shaking! The dust cloud! They craned their necks to peer inside the box.

Suddenly, a tiny face with over-size ears popped up.

"Nugget!" Dylan cried out joyfully.

The chinchilla's whiskers twitched. She clawed her way out of the box. Dylan scooped her up.

"She must have gotten a little muddy," he said. "Then she found a nice place to take a sand bath!"

Liz checked the damage in her diorama. "Oh boy. I might have to start over!" she said with a laugh.

The girls gathered around Dylan and Nugget. They took turns petting her gently. "Her fur is so soft!" Amy said.

Dylan looked so happy and relieved to have her back, safe and sound.

"So, Dylan," Liz said, a little unsure of how to phrase what she wanted to ask. "You can't really hear out of your right ear?"

Dylan smiled. "Well, usually I *can*. When I have my hearing aid in  that ear. But the battery died the day we moved, and I'm waiting for my new doctor to get the prescription."

Liz nodded, understanding. "Well, if you need any help until you get your prescription, we're all here for you!" she told him.

"Thanks, you guys," Dylan said. He looked around at each of them. "We barely know each other. But you've already really helped me out. Nugget, too."

Liz smiled. It was true—they barely knew Dylan. But she had a feeling they were going to get to know him!

Chapter 10

Diorama Day

On Friday, Mrs. Sienna's class handed in their dioramas. She asked each student to stand and show their work to the class.

"How did you choose your animal?" Mrs. Sienna asked them.

Amy said that she'd read about arctic wolves in her wildlife magazine. Drifts of cotton balls made her diorama look cold and snowy. "Arctic wolves have two layers of fur to keep them warm," Amy said.

Ellie's toucan diorama was alive with color. "Toucans are tropical birds like my Nana's parrot, Lenny," she said. "But guess what? They are not very good at flying. They mostly hop from branch to branch."

Marion held up her zebra diorama. "I chose zebras because they are related to horses," she said. "Did you know that zebra stripes are like human fingerprints? No two patterns are exactly alike."

Soon it was Dylan's turn. He explained that he had moved to Santa Vista from Colorado.

"That's why I chose the bighorn sheep," he said. "Where I used to live, we would see them along the road all the time."

Liz stood up to show her diorama.

She *had* made a new one, thanks to Nugget. But she was glad. This time, she had used darker blue paint to make deeper-looking water. She

had glued on clear glass beads to look like bubbles.

And for the octopus, Liz had wrapped a ball in metallic fabric. She had attached eight wide ribbons for the tentacles. Thin strips of bubble wrap on each tentacle looked like rows of suckers.

"Some octopuses have two hundred and forty suckers on *each* tentacle! They are really strong. Large suckers can hold up to thirty-five pounds!" Liz told the class. "One time, at the beach, I took care of a baby octopus that washed ashore.

That's how I got the idea to choose the octopus. They are so amazing!"

Mrs. Sienna winked at Liz. "Sometimes the best ideas take time to figure out," she said. "Right, Liz?"

"Yep," Liz said with a smile. "And sometimes they're right under your nose!"

119

Visit CritterClubBooks.com for activities, excerpts, and the series trailer!